C-2

Judith
n Pumpkin Smasher

The Halloween Pumpkin Smasher

The Halloween Pumpkin Smasher

by Judith St. George

Illustrated by Margot Tomes

G. P. Putnam's Sons/New York

Text copyright © 1978 by Judith St. George
Illustrations copyright © 1978 by Margot Tomes
All rights reserved. Published simultaneously in Canada
by General Publishing Co. Limited, Toronto.
Printed in the United States of America
Library of Congress Cataloging in Publication Data
St. George, Judith.
The Halloween pumpkin smasher.
Summary: Mary Grace and her imaginary friend
Nellie plan to find out who has been smashing all
the jack-o'-lanterns the week before Halloween.
[1. Halloween—fiction.   2. Mystery and
detective stories]   I. Tomes, Margot.   II. Title.
PZ7.S142Hal   [E]   77-26294
ISBN 0-399-20617-5
Fourth Impression

To Aunt Nellie,
who is also smart, brave and kind

Contents

1

The Meanest Man
on Grove Street

"Look at that, Nellie," I cried.

Nellie and I leaned over the Tylers' hedge. The Tylers' jack-o'-lantern had been smashed. Pieces of pumpkin lay all over their yard.

"Jinks, that's the fourth jack-o'-lantern smashed on Grove Street this week," I said.

Nellie and I had carved our jack-o'-lantern last night and set it in our tree house window. It had jagged teeth and an evil smile. It was beautiful. What if our jack-o'-lantern got smashed?

(9)

"Nellie, you and I have to find the pumpkin smasher before Halloween," I said. Halloween was only three days away.

Nellie agreed.

Nellie was my make-believe playmate, and I counted on her. I, Mary Grace Potts, had made Nellie up to be my very best friend. She was smart, brave and kind. Nellie had lots of time to think about the pumpkin smasher. After all, she didn't have to do chores or even go to school. Nellie didn't have to do anthing she didn't want to.

"Who is the pumpkin smasher, Nellie?" I asked.

Nellie frowned. She hunched up her shoulders. She made her big, blue eyes small and mean. She looked just like Mr. Norton.

"You're right, Nellie," I said. "Mr. Norton is the meanest man on Grove Street. Last Halloween when the Maple Street Gang hid his weathervane, he called the police. He doesn't like fun, and he hates Halloween. Mr. Norton must be the pumpkin smasher." (11)

Nellie and I decided to set a trap. We took a pumpkin from Mama's root cellar. We carried it to Mr. Norton's house way down at one end of the street. It was getting dark. The big oak tree stretched bare arms to the sky. The moon was a slice of pie overhead.

Mr. Norton's house had wings and porches and gables. The shutters were closed. The paint was peeling. It looked like a house where a pumpkin smasher would live. It looked like a house where ghosts would live, too.

Nellie and I put our pumpkin on the back porch.
When Mr. Norton came out to smash it, we would
catch him.

"What if Mr. Norton smashes us?" I asked Nellie.
Nellie was so brave. She just laughed.

We ran and hid behind a maple tree. We waited.
We watched. The wind tossed dry leaves across the
yard. Bats dipped and swooped over the barn. Mr.
Norton's house looked very dark. Electricity had just
come to Grove Street. Some people were afraid to use

it. Maybe Mr. Norton was afraid to use it, too. That must be why his house was so dark. Or maybe something terrible was going on inside.

That's what Nellie thought. She wanted us to take a look. I wanted us to wait some more. But Nellie was braver than me. I let Nellie lead the way up the back porch stairs. The top step creaked. Moon shadows danced on the house. An owl who-whooed in the tall oak tree. My knees were apple butter. My heart skipped rope in my chest.

Nellie and I peeked in the back window. A big black animal crouched in the kitchen, ready to spring.

"Run, Nellie," I whispered.

Nellie laughed.

I took a closer look. Nellie was so smart. The big black animal was Mr. Norton's big wood stove.

Nellie and I tiptoed around the porch and peeked in the parlor window. Giant white ghosts gathered in a circle.

"It's a band of ghosts," I squeaked. "They've killed Mr. Norton and moved into his house."

Nellie laughed.

I took a closer look. Nellie was so smart. They weren't ghosts at all. Big white sheets covered Mr. Norton's parlor furniture.

We tiptoed to the front porch.

Swish. A dark cloak blew across my path. It was a witch on a broomstick flying out the window. I started to run. Nellie stopped me. She held up the witch's cloak. It was a curtain blowing out a broken window.

Nellie was brave. I wasn't. I ran down Mr. Norton's front walk. I almost tripped on a big sign.

FOR SALE, said the sign.

For Sale!

No wonder the house was dark. No wonder sheets covered the parlor furniture. Mr. Norton had moved away. Mr. Norton couldn't be the pumpkin smasher. Now what? Now it was time to go home. Nellie and I would have to start all over again tomorrow.

2
The Maple Street Gang

The pumpkin smasher was still at work. That night, the McKays' jack-o'-lantern got smashed. When Nellie and I saw it, we ran to our tree house.

Whew, our jack-o'-lantern was still safe in the window.

I was worried. "Our jack-o'-lantern may be next, Nellie," I said.

Nellie had a plan. Nellie always had a plan. She pointed to the tree house ladder.

"You're right, Nellie," I said. "If we hide the (21)

ladder, then the pumpkin smasher can't climb up into our tree house."

Nellie and I took down the ladder. We hid it under a laurel bush.

"Now our jack-o'..." I stopped. I listened. I heard footsteps. Then I heard boys' voices. Nellie and I ducked behind the laurel bush.

"Are you sure no one saw us?" someone asked.

"Naw, we're home free," a voice answered.

Nellie poked her head around the laurel bush. I poked my head around Nellie. I saw Horace Tucker, Willard Jones, Abner Harris, Lem Booth and Bert Higgins sneaking past our tree house. It was the Maple Street Gang.

"My pa would take a strap to me if he knew what we was up to," Horace Tucker said.

"Aw, we only do it once a year," Willard Jones answered.

Last Halloween, the Maple Street Gang put a cow in the church belfry. They soaped up every window on Grove Street, *and* hid Mr. Norton's weathervane. The Maple Street Gang were troublemakers. They must be the pumpkin smashers.

Nellie thought so, too. She jumped up to follow them.

(24)   "Don't go, Nellie," I begged.

The Maple Street Gang was tough. Yesterday they put a frog in the teacher's lunch pail. Last week they locked Freddie Cole in the woodshed and left him there all night. They said if anyone spied on them, they would "tie 'em into a pretzel and roll 'em down Maple Street." Everyone was afraid of the Maple Street Gang.

Nellie wasn't. She ran after them. What could I do? I ran after Nellie. My knees were apple butter. My heart skipped rope in my chest.

Nellie and I followed the Maple Street Gang through the woods. I stepped on a dry twig. It snapped. Bert Higgins stopped. He looked back. Nellie and I froze. Bert didn't see us. He ran after his friends. They kept going until they reached the back of Mr. Brown's barn. Nellie and I followed a safe distance behind.

"We got to stamp 'em all out," we heard Abner Harris say.

"We got to light 'em before we can stamp 'em out," That was Lem Booth.

Nellie and I were right. The Maple Street Gang was smashing pumpkins.

Nellie nodded toward the open barn boor. I nodded back toward home. I didn't want to be tied into a pretzel and rolled down Maple Street.

Nellie was braver than me. She ran into the barn. What could I do? I followed her. We smelled smoke.

"We have to get out, Nellie," I cried. "They're setting the barn on fire."

Nellie shook her head. She was looking out the back barn window. I looked out the window, too.

The Maple Street Gang sat in a circle. Horace Tucker's face was green. Abner Harris was coughing. Willard Jones' eyes were watering. The Maple Street Gang wasn't smashing pumpkins. They had pulled the silk off ears of corn and were smoking it like tobacco. They all looked sick.

What a sight. Nellie and I hadn't caught the pumpkin smashers, but we had a good laugh on the Maple Street Gang.

3

The Blue and Gold 1909 Model T Ford Touring Car

Nellie and I stared at the Browns' jack-o'-lantern. It was smashed all over their yard. Jinks! That was pumpkin number six. Tomorrow was Halloween and Nellie and I still hadn't found the pumpkin smasher.

BANK! BANG! CHANGITY! POOOWWW!

It was gunshots on Grove Street.

Nellie and I ducked behind the Browns' hitching post.

BANG! BANG! The shots came closer.

Nellie and I peeked out. It wasn't gunshots at all. It was Mr. Simpson's automobile.

(29)

Mr. Simpson had just bought a blue and gold 1909 Model T Ford Touring Car. It was the first automobile on Grove Street. Grandpa said it was a danger to life and limb. Mama said the fumes poisoned the air. All the dogs barked when Mr. Simpson drove by. The horses bucked and reared. The cats ran and hid. I felt like hiding, too. Mr. Simpson was a terrible driver.

Nellie and I watched Mr. Simpson turn into his barn.

(31)

POOOWWW! came one last backfire.

Nellie snapped her fingers. She had an idea. Mr. Simpson was such a bad driver. He was smashing all the jack-o'-lanterns with his brand new automobile.

Nellie and I decided on a plan.

"We'll look on the fender of the car," I said. "If we find pieces of pumpkin, we'll know Mr. Simpson's (32) Model T Ford is the Grove Street pumpkin smasher."

Nellie and I tiptoed into Mr. Simpson's barn. Mr. Simpson's 1909 blue and gold Model T Ford Touring Car was parked inside. It had brass lamps, a windshield, a shiny bulb horn and a folding canvas top. Mr. Simpson was very proud of it. He said he would horsewhip anyone who touched it. I believed him.

I guess Nellie didn't. She climbed in the back seat. She sat up tall and straight. She waved like a queen. I climbed in beside her. I sat up tall and straight too. Nellie and I waved to the crowds.

"I'll be back in an hour, dear."

Jinks! It was Mr. Simpson. He was right outside the barn door. Nellie and I jumped onto the floor of the back seat. We heard the barn door open. Mr. Simpson cranked the starter.

Vrooom! Vrooom! Vrooom!

Mr. Simpson climbed in the driver's seat.

I hoped he wouldn't see Nellie and me. I had never been horsewhipped and didn't want to start now. My knees were apple butter. My heart skipped rope in my chest. But Nellie was brave. She held my hand for courage.

Bangity! Bang! Bang! POOWW!

I shut my eyes tight. We bumpity-bumped out of the barn.

POOWW!

"Good morning, Mr. Potts," Mr. Simpson called.

That must be Grandpa.

"Get a horse," came the answer.

That was Grandpa all right.

Now we were picking up speed. Dust flew. Dogs barked. We spun around the corner of Grove Street. We would all be killed. I would rather be horsewhipped. I jumped up to call for help, but Nellie pushed me down.

Thumpity...thump...thump...

Something was wrong. We were jerking like a jackrabbit. It was the end.

No, the automobile bucked to a stop.

"Confound it," Mr. Simpson swore. "It couldn't be another breakdown. This blasted car has been in the repair shop all week."

We heard Mr. Simpson climb out and slam his door. Nellie and I looked over the front seat. The hood of the automobile was up. Mr. Simpson's head was under the hood.

Nellie and I didn't need a plan. We knew just what to do. We opened the back door and jumped out.

Nellie and I ran all the way home. We fell down on our porch swing. We were breathing hard. Nellie looked pale. She thought I looked pale, too. We had a right to be pale. Mr. Simpson had been driving thirty miles an hour.

As we rested on the swing, I began to think. All the jack-o'-lanterns on Grove Street had been smashed this week. But Mr. Simpson's automobile was in the (37) repair shop all week. That meant the Model T Ford Touring Car couldn't be the pumpkin smasher.

Nellie and I still hadn't found the pumpkin smasher, but I had figured out who *wasn't* the pumpkin smasher. For once, I, Mary Grace Potts, had been just as smart as Nellie. Maybe even smarter.

4

🍂 The Pumpkin Smasher

It was Halloween.

I was an elf. Nellie was a fairy princess. Nellie and I were going to a corn-popping party. But we had something to do first. We had to make sure our jack-o'-lantern was still safe. We headed for our tree house.

Black clouds darkened the sky. Wet leaves were slippery underfoot. It was a time for witches and ghosts and goblins. Nellie and I reached the tree house. (39)

I pointed to the window. "Look, Nellie, our jack-
o'-lantern is safe."

Nellie frowned. She put her fingers to her lips.

"What is it, Nellie? I don't hear anything," I said.

Thump... thump...

This time I heard it, too.

(40) Then, crash! bang!

A terrible smashing and thumping came from inside our tree house. Nellie pulled me down behind the laurel bush. I looked at Nellie. Nellie looked at me. We had the same thought. The pumpkin smasher must be in our tree house. But the tree house ladder was still hidden under the laurel bush. There was no way to reach the tree house unless the pumpkin smasher was a witch... or a ghost... or a goblin....

Thumpity! Thump! Crash!

The noises were getting louder. Maybe a witch would fly out and snatch up Nellie and me with bony fingers. Or a ghost would swoop down and turn us to stone. Or a goblin would tie us up and carry us away.

I wondered what Mama would say when I didn't come home. I wondered what my teacher would say when I didn't show up at school. My knees were apple butter. My heart double-skipped rope in my chest. Nellie looked scared, too.

There wasn't much light. It was hard to see. Rain was beginning to fall. Suddenly a face popped up in the tree house window. It wore a mask just like mine. *Swoosh.* The candle went out.

CRASH!

Nellie and I heard our jack-'o-lantern smash on the tree house floor. I wanted to call for help, but my

(41)

voice wouldn't work. I wanted to run home, but my feet wouldn't move.

We waited for more crashing and thumping. The tree house was silent. All we heard was the rain tiptapping on the roof. The wind moaned through the woods.

Nellie grabbed my arm. Her blue eyes were frightened. Nellie was counting on me. Jinks, I had to think of something.

I thought. I studied the tree house. I looked at the ladder still under the laurel bush. An idea was coming to me.

I stood up. I picked up the tree house ladder. I walked out from the laurel bush and leaned the ladder against the tree. My idea was getting bigger and bigger. I waved for Nellie to follow, but Nellie shook her head. She was afraid to come.

Slowly I climbed the ladder to the tree house. Were witches brewing smashed pumpkin with snakeskins and toads? Were ghosts making plans to haunt Grove Street? Were goblins working their black magic? I didn't think so, but I wasn't sure.

Maybe I should turn back. Nellie waved at me to turn back. My heart thumped at me to turn back. My knees shook at me to turn back. My idea told me to keep going. Now I was on the tree house porch. I closed my eyes tight. I took a deep breath. I opened them.

The tree house was a sight. The table was turned over. The cookie jar was broken. The chair was broken, too. Pieces of pumpkin lay everywhere, and there in the corner was the pumpkin smasher.

My knees unlocked. My voice came back. I laughed. My idea had been right after all.

I backed down the ladder. It was time to go to our corn-popping party. Nellie hadn't helped, but it didn't matter. We were best friends. Besides, I liked the feeling that I, Mary Grace Potts, could be smart and brave. I could be kind, too. I was quiet as I (45) climbed down the ladder. I wanted the pumpkin smasher to enjoy his own Halloween party.